# This book belongs

to: _____

May books become your "treasured friends".

# The Tale of Tumeleng

## Ms. Ryke Leigh Douglas

Illustrations by Angel dela Peña

Copyright © Ms. Ryke Leigh Douglas.

All rights reserved. No part of this book may be reproduced in any form or by any electronic or mechanical means, including information storage and retrieval systems, without permission in writing from the publisher, except by reviewers, who may quote brief passages in a review.

ISBN:   978-1-64826-518-1   (Paperback Edition)
ISBN:   978-1-64826-519-8   (Hardcover Edition)
ISBN:   978-1-64826-517-4   (E-book Edition)

Some characters and events in this book are fictitious. Any similarity to real persons, living or dead, is coincidental and not intended by the author.


Book Ordering Information

Phone Number: 347-901-4929 or 347-901-4920
Email: info@globalsummithouse.com
Global Summit House
www.globalsummithouse.com

Printed in the United States of America

FOR MY GRANDCHILDREN

# SOMEWHERE IN AFRICA

It is the middle of a very black night in the rainforest of Africa. Jabari, an adult ten-foot tall, six-ton bull elephant with legs as big as porch posts, is standing very still. He appears to be sleeping. However, he is very much awake, and listening very carefully. In the distance, he can hear the loud whooping calls of several hyenas as they call back and forth. Jabari knows they are creeping closer and closer to him, and he knows why!

Behind him, deeper in the rainforest an important event is taking place. A calf is about to be born into Jabari's small family herd. The hyenas know that the cows are distracted with the new baby's arrival. It will be easier to snatch one of the younger calves, who may have strayed too far from its mother's side.

The birth of a calf is always an important and joyful event for an elephant herd, but this one is very special for Jabari. He has been waiting two long years for the calf's arrival. He is the baby's father. Male elephants leave the family unit when they are teenagers to live alone or to pal around with a band of other bulls. Although Jabari no longer lives with his family, he sometimes visits to show his affection for his mother, his aunt cows, and his mate, Ayanna. Tonight however, he is helping to protect the baby and his family unit. He is guarding the path that leads to the waterhole where the Matriarch cow, Zonda, the female leader of the herd, has gathered the cows and young calves in a circle to await the baby's arrival.

## DANGER LURKS

Jabari makes low rumbling sounds to alert the cows that the hyenas are getting closer! His ears flare out from the sides of his head. He raises his head and plants his feet far apart and firmly on the ground. His tail raises and his trunk is unfurled. He is ready to deal with the unwelcome hyenas.

Suddenly the big elephant turns, and with a loud bellow, charges into the undergrowth of bushes, shrubs, and small trees that lines both sides of the path. He tosses branches, grass, and small shrubs out of his way.

Jabari plunges his eight-foot long tusks into the unlucky hyena who thought he could sneak past him. He lifts the hyena with his trunk and tosses him toward the other two hyenas that are rapidly retreating with their tails curled below their bellies in fear.

The soon to be father waits patiently until he is satisfied that the hyenas are no longer a threat to his family, then he slowly lumbers back along the ancient elephant path to join the cows.

It is almost morning now. Towering treetops provide a thick canopy of leaves and branches that cover the forest floor like a ceiling. Sunbeams sneak through small openings and make the leaves gleam and sparkle. Drops of water cling like shiny beads on the branches and vines. All through the jungle, the animals are beginning a new day. Hundreds of colorful butterflies flutter in the early dawn mist. Spiders are repairing the holes made in their webs by a few rain showers during the night.

Grunts, growls, and roars, chatters, whistles, and songs, snarls, squawks, and squeals begin to fill the early morning quiet.

Before long, Jabari hears loud, swishing, crunching, and snapping sounds behind him. His band of bull elephants is following him to the waterhole to welcome the new baby.

When the bulls arrive, the cows are standing in a ring around the mother elephant and her calf. Ayanna very gently prods the baby girl to its feet with her trunk and her feet. Although the calf tries hard, her legs are wobbly. It takes almost an hour, and many shaky attempts before the baby manages to stand, wiggle her ears and shake her tail. She is almost as tall as a yardstick and weighs close to 250 pounds!

# A JOYFUL WELCOMING

Now there is another problem. Ayanna is trying to guide her to drink some milk, but the calf's floppy, wiggly trunk keeps getting in the way, and she doesn't know what to do with it. Just as babies have to learn how to walk, elephants have to learn how to use their trunks. Later, the calf will learn that its trunk is a very useful tool, but right now, she just keeps stepping on it and swishing it around.

After many attempts, the rest of the elephants proudly watch as the newborn enjoys her first meal. They begin to trumpet loudly to welcome the baby into the herd. When it is quiet again, Ayanna proudly introduces her new daughter, "This is Tumeleng, her name means joy. One day she may be your matriarch," she tells them. "I need all of your help to teach her everything she will need to know to be a good leader."

Elephants are very respectful of one another so, Jabari waits until Ayanna is finished speaking and then slowly approaches Tumeleng. He gently rubs his long trunk over her back to show his affection for her. Then one by one, all of the elephants take turns inspecting and welcoming Tumeleng. They gently rub and touch her with their trunks. They make soft low sounds to show their approval and acceptance. They will love and help to care for her.

Before Jabari leaves to join his band of bulls, he tells Ayanna how proud he is of his new daughter.

# THE WATERHOLE

Late that afternoon, Zonda calls the aunties together for an important reason. As the matriarch speaks, the cows listen respectfully.

"I know this waterhole is nearly useless to us and we need to look for another source of water and better food, but I think we should remain here for two more days. It will give Tumeleng some time to gain strength for our journey and to learn how to deal with her wiggly trunk a little better. It will also benefit our other young calves."

The cows all agree that Zonda's suggestion is a very wise one. They will stay for two more days.

Early in the evening on the second day, Zonda gathers the cows together again and tells them, "Be ready to leave early tomorrow morning before the sun is up. It will be cooler to travel and we can get further. Make sure you take your baths!"

The next morning, Tumeleng wakes up to the sounds of the herd having a wonderful time, splashing, spraying, and squirting themselves and each other as they wash in the water that is still left in the waterhole.

When they get out of the water, Tumeleng watches as they begin spraying each other all over with the dust, dirt, and mud from the sides of the waterhole.

When the others are finished bathing, Ayanna gently pushes Tumeleng into the water at a spot where the baby can easily stand. She sprays her with water and rubs her clean with her trunk. After Ayanna has showered herself, she smears them both with mud too.

Now the whole herd is wearing mud coats!

In the weeks ahead, Tumeleng will begin to understand the importance of the mud bath ritual when Ayanna explains, "The mud will help protect our skin from getting sunburned. It also keeps insects from biting us, especially ticks and mosquitoes that carry diseases and can make us sick."

Just before they are ready to leave, Jabari visits with Ayanna to tell her with gestures and low sounds, "I will never be too far away from the herd so that you can call me if you need help, and I will visit when I can." Then he affectionately and gently rubs Tumeleng with his trunk. Before lumbering back into the forest to join his band of bulls, he entwines his trunk with Ayanna's trunk.

When she is sure everyone is in line, Zonda signals she is ready to begin by lifting her trunk high in the air to sniff and smell the air for water, food, and danger. She leads them slowly over the ancient maze of paths that her mother has taught her were used every year by generations of elephants before them. Tumeleng stays between Ayanna's big legs most of the time. Unlike most animals, elephants are not born with all of the skills they need to survive in their rainforest world. Ayanna encourages Tumeleng to peek out, watch, and listen. Tumeleng quickly learns that all the adult cows are her aunties and the calves are her sisters, brothers, and cousins. She also discovers that she needs to listen, obey, and respect all of the aunties as well as Ayanna.

The cows follow Zonda in single file with the young calves either underneath their stomachs or walking beside them. The most important job the aunties have is to protect the young calves, but they also work at keeping order and harmony in the herd. They talk to each other using sounds and gestures. They are polite, kind, and helpful to one another. Each adult has a job to do besides protecting the young ones. A number walk in the middle of the herd and make sure the calves are staying close. A few walk at the front of the line with the Matriarch, Zonda. Several adults follow at the end of the line to watch for enemies like tigers, lions, leopards, hyenas, wild dogs and the most dangerous of all, human hunters, called poachers.

Zonda stops often to let the adults rest and graze while the young calves nurse, rest or play. Whenever they come to a waterhole, the herd stops to drink, wash away bugs, and cool themselves off as they splash and squirt each other in play. The aunties take turns grazing, watching for danger, and making sure the older calves stay close by. Each one only naps for a short time.

The journey never ends because it is not safe for the herd to stay in one place for very long.

## WHAT TO DO?

Zonda continues to lead the herd at a slow pace for several weeks, but one morning after traveling just a short distance, the herd comes to an abrupt halt. A very old tree has fallen right across the middle of the path. Broken branches are sticking out in every direction. The brush is too thick on both sides of the path for them to go around it. Even if the cows could remove some of the branches and climb over it themselves, the calves are all too little to climb over it. The adult cows try to figure out what to do. All of the young elephants stand quietly in a group and watch and wait. Their eyes show fear and hold a question that Tumeleng bravely asks: "Will they leave us here?"

"No you just watch and see," Ayanna replies.

The nervous calves wait quietly as several of the aunties work together. First, they pull out some of the smaller trees, bushes, and plants along one side of the path and toss them further into the forest. Next, they push, pull, shove, tug, heave, and roll the huge log off to the side of the trail.

The wise leader wastes no time getting the herd moving again. The days have become very hot, and Zonda knows that without enough drinking water every day the herd will not survive. She must keep them moving from waterhole to waterhole as quickly as the youngest ones are able to travel.

## LEARNING TO SURVIVE

While they are walking, Ayanna lovingly and patiently teaches Tumeleng and continues to keep her in the shade of her stomach. Once in a while she allows her to walk right next to her so she can learn how to talk and play with the other young calves.

By the time she is five months old, Tumeleng has learned how to roll up her trunk so she can drink her mother's milk without tripping over the annoying, floppy thing. This is a very important skill! Tumeleng needs to drink close to 20 pints of Ayanna's rich milk every day for several years or until she is able to forage and graze completely on her own.

It takes many more months for Tumeleng to discover that the trunk she thought was a nuisance is also a valuable tool. She learns to use it like a straw to suck up water to put into her mouth, or spray herself with water to cool off. It works great for scratching an itch too! Best of all, she discovers she can have fun with it.

Ayanna plays with Tumeleng and some of the other younger calves. She drops nuts, twigs and leaves down on the ground so they can practice using the finger-like tips of their trunks for small tasks like picking a berry off a bush or a juicy leaf off a tree when they are older

In the months ahead, while the herd continues its endless search for food and water, Tumeleng learns other ways to use her trunk. By now, she knows flapping her ears will help keep her cool. However, she has also learned how to trumpet and make other noises with her trunk. The most important lesson Ayanna wants her to learn, is the hardest one for Tumeleng. She just cannot remember to stay close and not wander away. Over and over again, Ayanna and the aunties remind her, "Baby elephants are easily killed by lions, snakes, and hyenas or captured by elephant hunters." Tumeleng, just like most baby elephants is curious, and though she doesn't mean to, she forgets about the lions, tigers, snakes, and hyenas. She doesn't even know what they are!

Elephant herds traveling along the maze of ancient paths often meet another herd of friends or relatives. These gentle, sociable giants will raise their heads and greet each other in friendship with loud trumpeting rumbles, growls, and bellows while running toward one another. They show their affection for one another by entwining their trunks, clicking their tusks, and flapping their ears. They also touch, embrace, rub, and caress each other with their trunks.

It is during one of these social events that Tumeleng wanders away from Ayanna and the herd. While Ayanna is excitedly greeting an old friend, a colorful butterfly lands briefly on Tumeleng's trunk and, then flutters away. Tumeleng wonders where it is going. Without a thought about lions, tigers, snakes, or hyenas, Tumeleng follows the tiny creature. She pokes her trunk into the thick undergrowth of brush and vines on the jungle floor. The butterfly disappears. Where has it gone? She keeps looking and searching. Suddenly a huge fruit pod hits her on the head and bounces to the ground in front of her. This causes her to cry, "What was that?"

# STRANGE SOUNDS

Tumeleng is just beginning to feel brave enough to poke the odd thing with her trunk, when she hears chirping sounds coming from somewhere. Looking up she sees a ball of twigs hanging from a branch above her head. Now she is really curious... maybe that is where the butterfly has gone, she thinks. She forgets about the fruit pod and begins trying to reach the ball of twigs with her trunk, but another strange sound stops her.

On a branch above her head, and below the ball of twigs is a five-foot long hissing creature. Tumeleng has interrupted a dangerous and poisonous boom slang snake as he is about to enjoy his noon meal. The ball of twigs is a nest, and inside are four baby weaverbirds. Now the snake is not only hungry, he is also very angry! He opens his mouth and slowly inches toward Tumeleng. The baby elephant watches as the snake inches closer and closer. Its tongue is darting in and out of its gaping mouth. HISS! HISS!

Tumeleng senses she is in real danger! She squeals in terror and knows she should run, but she is so frightened she cannot move!

Suddenly, Tumeleng hears an ear-piercing bellow followed by the loud sounds of branches, bushes, and trees crunching, snapping, and cracking. The ground vibrates as Ayanna comes thundering and crashing through the jungle to rescue her daughter. Ayanna wraps her trunk around the branch the boom slang is on and breaks it off the tree. She tosses it high into the air with the snake still clinging to it. It lands in the middle of an almost dried up waterhole and sinks out of sight into the mud.

Tumeleng is so very glad to see her mother, but a glance at her mother's face tells her that Ayanna is very disturbed with her. Tumeleng is ashamed and embarrassed. How many times has she been warned to stay close to the herd and here she is, well she has no idea where she is, or which direction to take to get back to the herd. She hangs her head and slowly follows Ayanna back to the safety of the worried, waiting herd. Ayanna does not scold her. She knows that Tumeleng has learned a valuable survival lesson.

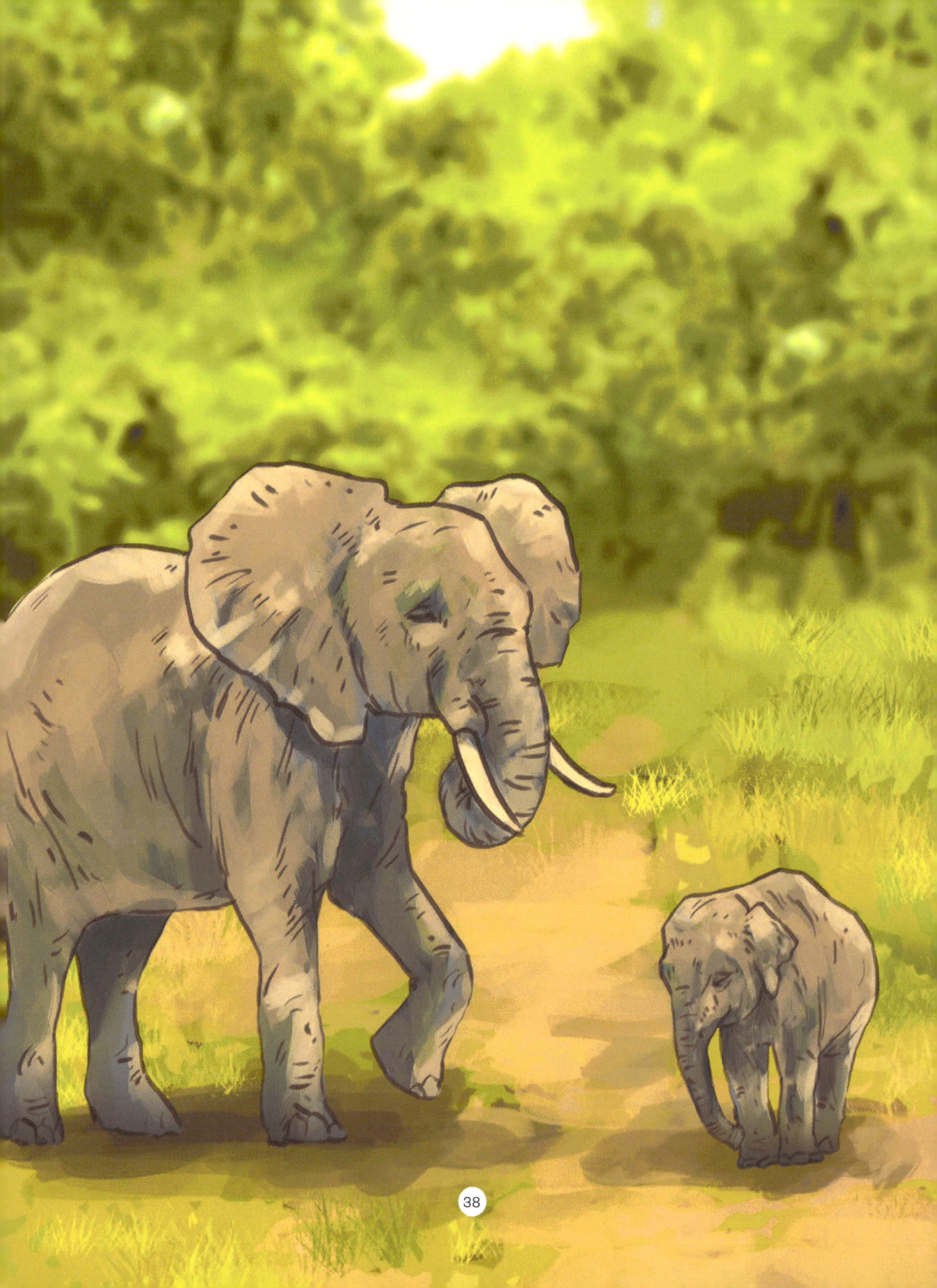

# RAFIKI

One very hot afternoon, while the herd is resting in the shade of some trees, Jabari comes for a visit, but he is not alone. Walking beside him is a young bull calf a year or two older than Tumeleng. After speaking briefly with the Matriarch, Zonda, Jabari introduces the young bull to the herd, "This is Rafiki. His name means friend. I found him wandering alone in the forest searching for his mother. I did not find any other family close by, so I think he may be an orphan. Zonda has given permission for him to travel with you. Hopefully, we will meet his family herd along the way, and he can be reunited with them."

Ayanna, Tumeleng, and the rest of the herd quickly welcome the young bull with elephant trunk hugs and gentle rubs.

For several weeks, Rafiki stays very close to Ayanna and his new friend Tumeleng. He does not play with the older calves even though he is old enough to join them. Sometimes, Rafiki sits by himself and makes soft, moaning squeals, and Tumeleng cannot get him to talk to her or join in the game Ayanna plays with them. "You need to respect Rafiki's wish to be alone." Ayanna explains, "He is feeling sad, and missing his mother and his family herd." Many more weeks pass before Rafiki finally begins to play with the older calves.

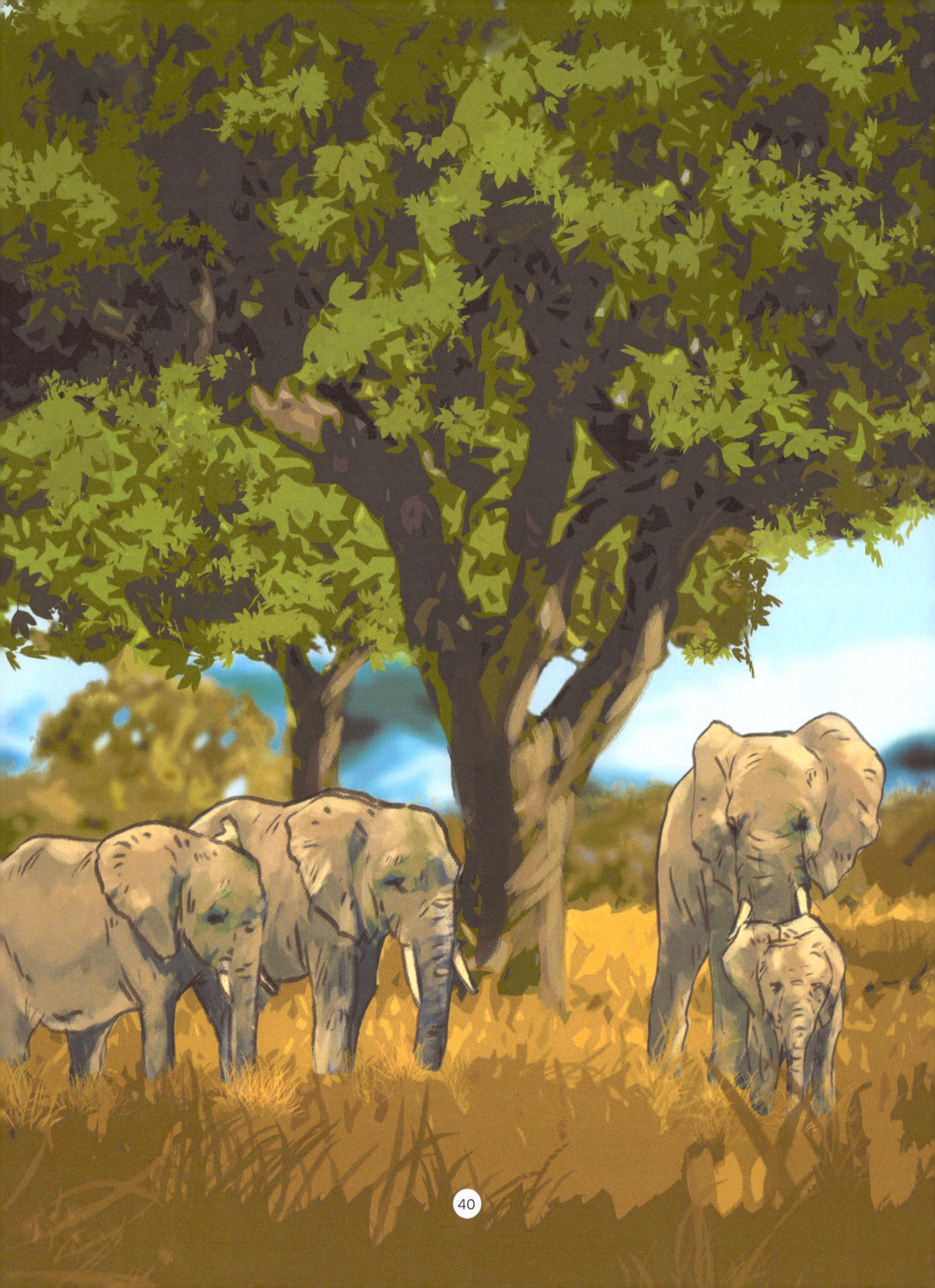

Baby elephants learn to swim at an early age. When the herd reaches a waterhole, they don't just drink and wash off the bugs, dust, and dirt. They play, swim, roll, splash, squirt each other, and even the adults just have a wonderful fun time. The calves will play in the mud playground all day if their mothers will let them.

Tumeleng loves to play a game with Ayanna. She lays on her back in the water along with several of the other calves so just the tops of their trunks and the soles of their feet show. Ayanna pretends she doesn't know which one is Tumeleng for a while. Then she wraps her trunk around Tumeleng's trunk, and tugs so Tumeleng knows Ayanna has found her.

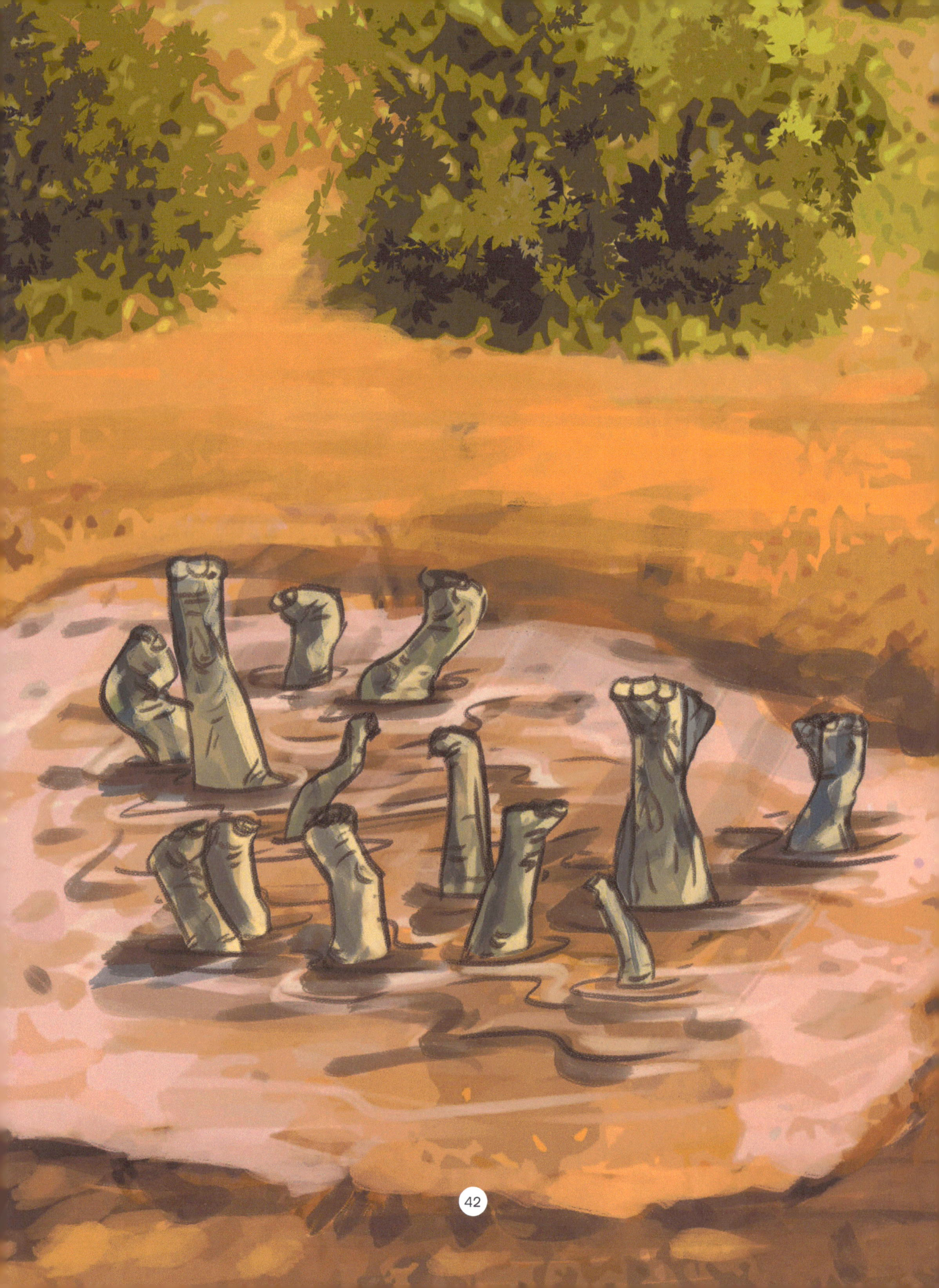

# A WARNING AND A PROMISE

As the months pass, and the herd continues its endless search for food and water, Jabari often visits to show his affection and concern for Ayanna and Tumeleng and Rafiki too.

Ayanna proudly tells him, "Our daughter learns very quickly and is always curious about what is happening around her. She watches and listens. I have even begun to teach her which plants and fruits are safe for her to eat." However, when Jabari mentions to Ayanna that it might soon be time to give Tumeleng freedom to play with the older calves, Ayanna does not agree. Even though she knows that baby elephants learn many things from each other, Ayanna tells Jabari, "I don't think she is ready yet."

"Tumeleng is not like the other girl calves that are more timid. She is so interested and anxious to learn about everything that she worries us. The aunties and I have to remind her constantly not to wander too far away from the herd. This week she gave us a real scare," and she tells Jabari about the boom slang. So before Jabari heads back to join his band of bulls, he sternly warns Tumeleng, "Always stay close to your mother and your aunts! There are too many dangers."

"I will!" Tumeleng promises.

# GROWING UP

Tumeleng is so excited. For months now, she has been begging to play with the older calves. Just this morning, Ayanna has given her permission.

At first, she is shy and timid about joining the group because most of them are males. But she is warmly welcomed when their trunks entwine with hers. and is quickly rolling small logs and tossing sticks and nuts back and forth with them. A favorite game is to chase another calf and pull its tail hard! It doesn't take long for Tumeleng to decide she enjoys this game the most. However, the day she pulls and chews on the tail of one of the auntie cows, is the day she earns her first real scolding from Ayanna for showing disrespect to an adult. She receives several trunk smacks on her rump, and for several days, she has to stay underneath Ayanna and watch and wish.

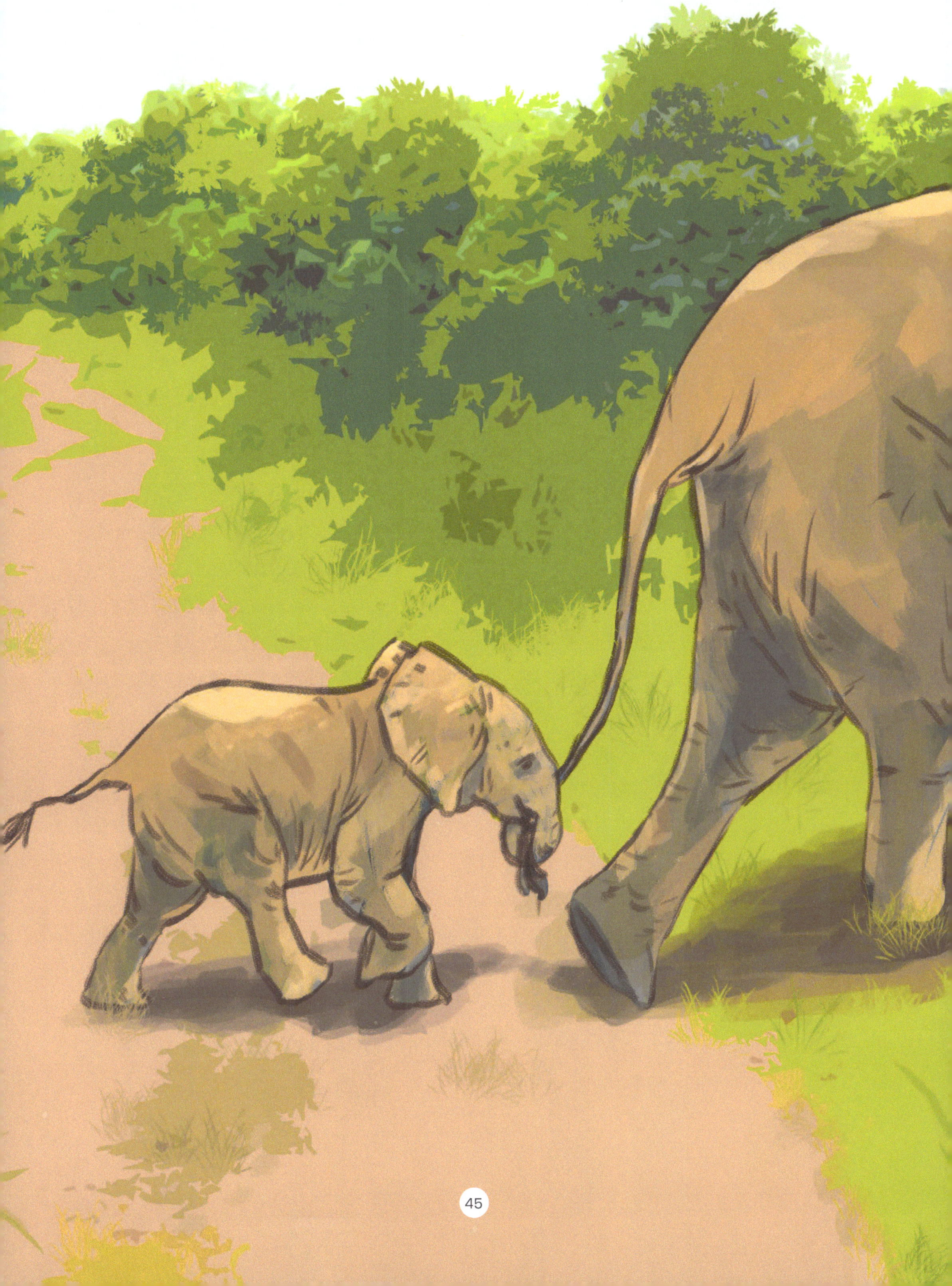

Tumeleng is really a good calf and she tries to remember Jabari's warning, but it is hard to do when she is having so much fun!

One afternoon she races across a clearing in the jungle trying to out-run Rafiki, and suddenly she is flying through the air! She lands with a loud frightened squeal at the bottom of a ditch. She looks at the steep sides of the ditch and knows she will not be able to climb out herself.

For the second time in her young life, Tumeleng is very afraid. How is she going to get out? She just sits and cries big tears. The next time she looks up, she sees that Rafiki has run to tell Ayanna who is looking down at her with a puzzled, worried expression. Tumeleng realizes that her mother does not know how to help her. Soon the whole herd is standing at the edge of the ditch staring down at her. Tumeleng is embarrassed and puts her head down so no one can see the tears in her eyes. A while later, Tumeleng bravely looks up again. She can see the Matriarch, Zonda, and Ayanna talking. Zonda is rubbing Ayanna with her trunk and making low sounds to comfort her. Suddenly, Ayanna begins making shrieking screams. They are sounds Tumeleng has never heard before. Then her mother begins stamping her feet on the ground. Tumeleng can feel the ground shaking slightly and she is thinking mother must be very angry with me! It will be dark soon. If the rest of the herd leaves, will she have to leave me here? Her thoughts make her shiver and shake with fear.

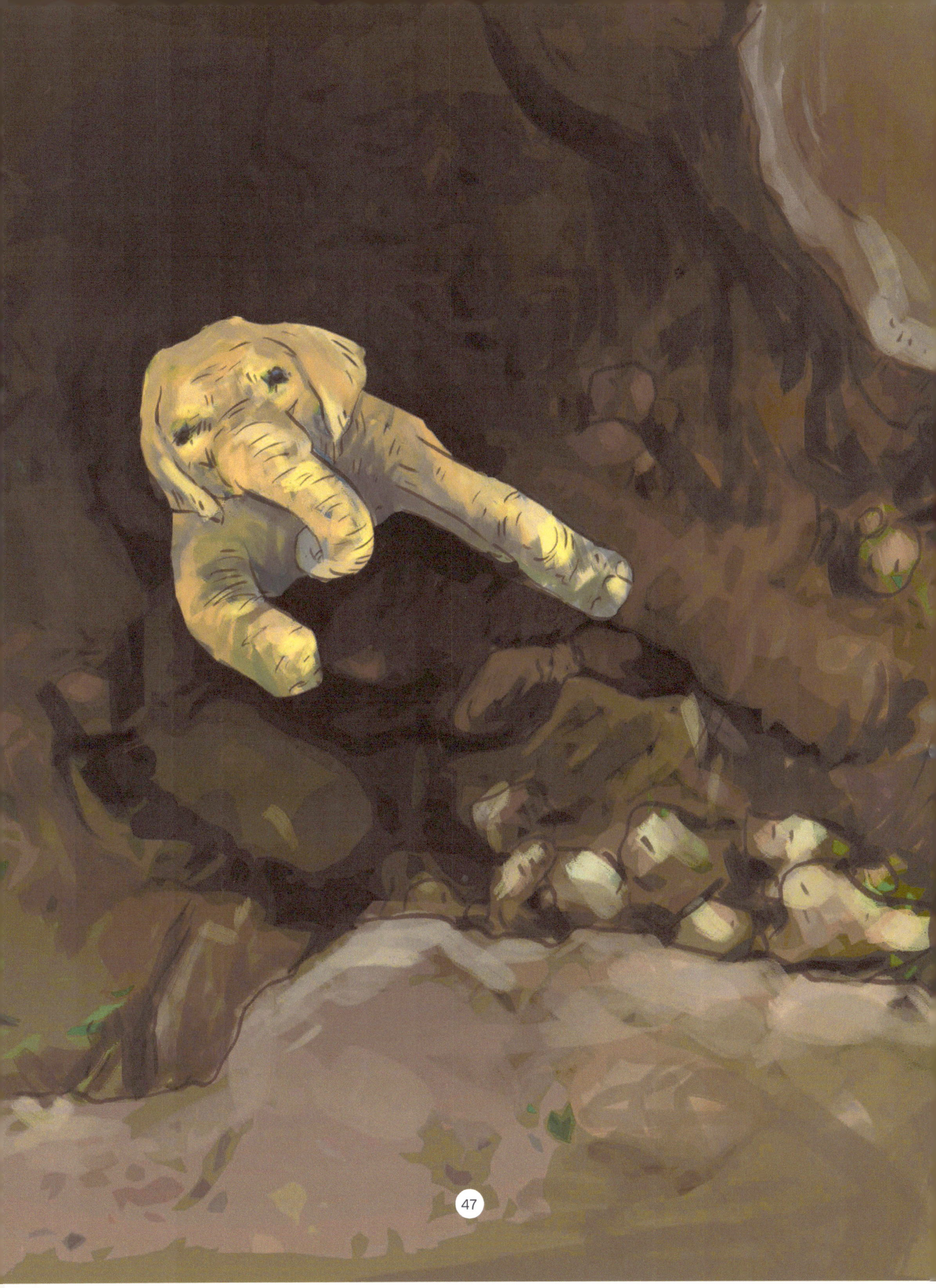

Suddenly, Jabari appears at the edge and peers down at his trapped daughter too. He looks soooo big from where Tumeleng is sitting at the bottom of the ditch, and Tumeleng is afraid. Will he be very angry with her for her foolishness?

To her surprise, Jabari just reaches down with his very long trunk and wraps it around Tumeleng's middle. With very little effort, he lifts her out of the ditch and gently sets her on the ground in front of Ayanna. Then he softly rubs her head with his trunk and says quietly "Remember, I told you, there are many dangers to watch out for. This is a poacher's ditch," he tells her. Then he lumbers back into the forest and although he is gone from their sight, both Ayanna and Tumeleng know he will not be too far away.

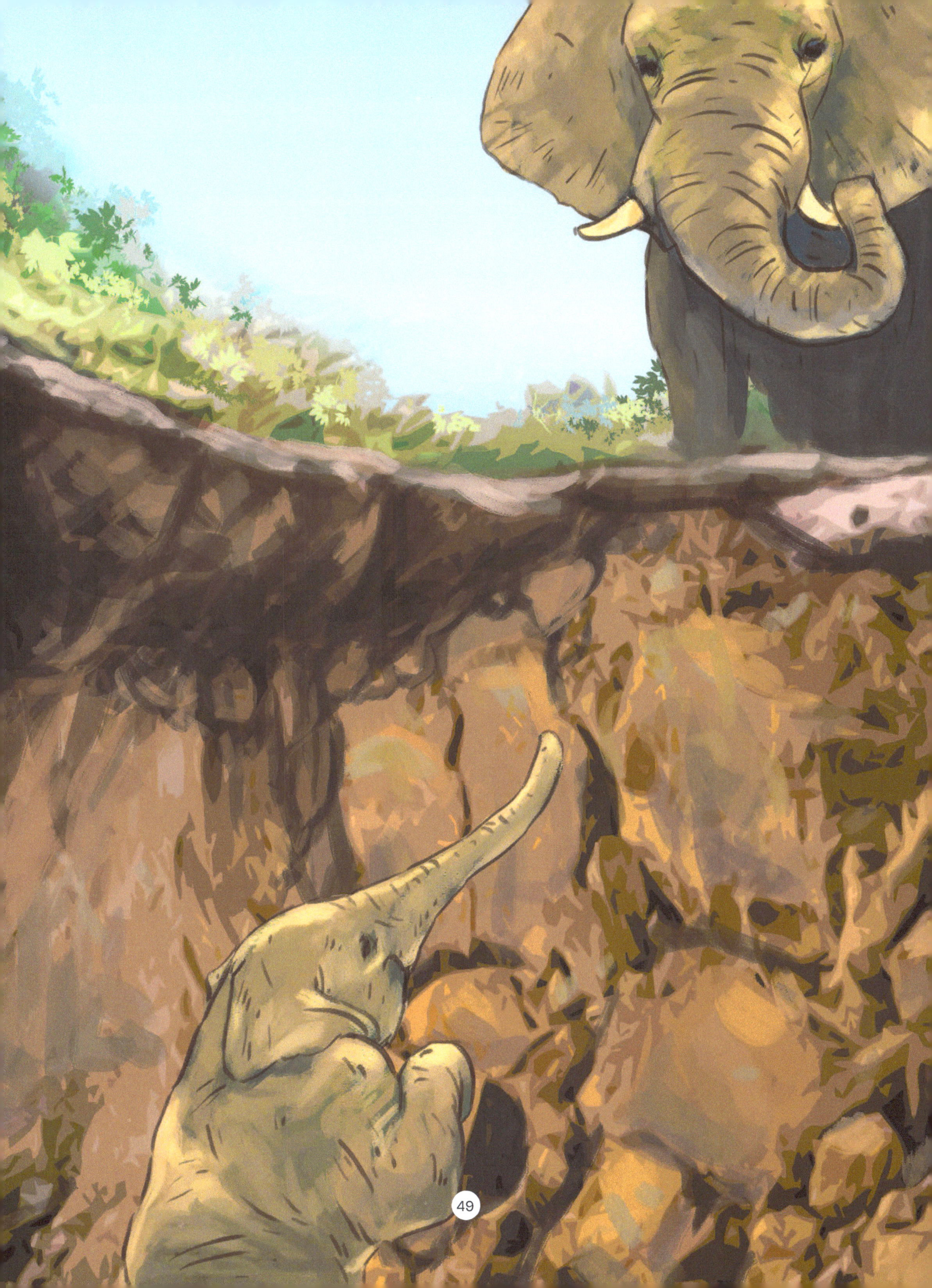

# A SAD DAY

They are right. Just a few days later, Jabari appears again. Ayanna can tell from the look on his face that something is very wrong. "I have some sad news," he tells the herd when they gather around him. "I have found the bodies of some of our friends, a herd we have met many times before. Poachers have cruelly killed them. Their tusks were removed and taken away."

Zonda, gathers her frightened and sad family together and they slowly follow Jabari. As they get closer to where Jabari has discovered the deceased family, Zonda and the rest of the adults begin to make loud, rumbling sounds. They form a circle and stand quietly to mourn the lost family in respectful silence. After a time, they begin to circle the bones, tenderly touching them with a foot or their trunk. Some gently pick up a bone and hold it for a while.

For the next two days, members of Zonda's family take turns covering the bodies with dirt, leaves, and tree branches to create a resting place.

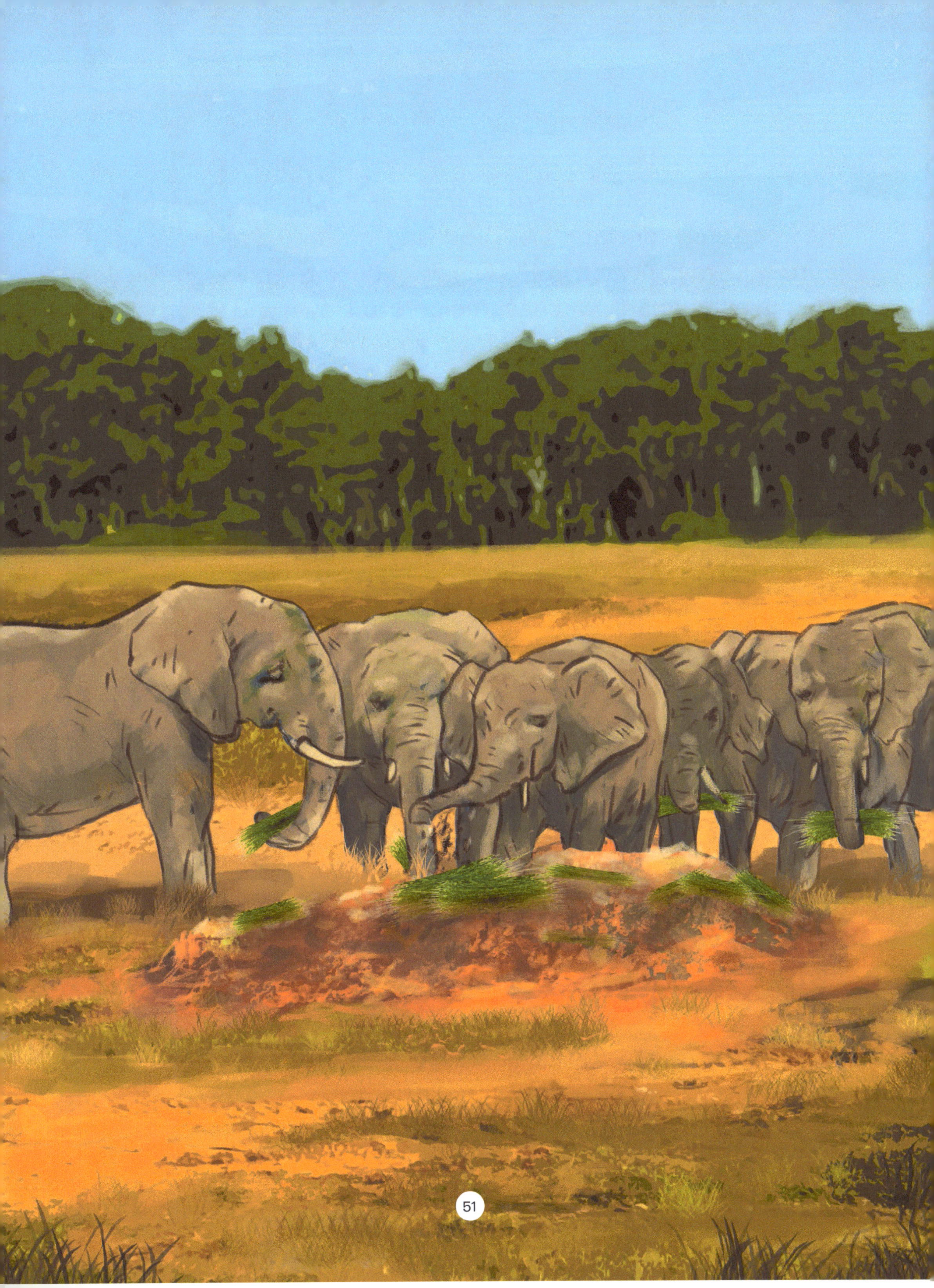

On the morning of the third day, Zonda raises her trunk high in the air to sniff for water and food, and the herd continues on its journey. Tumeleng and Rafiki wisely choose to walk right beside Ayanna and Jabari, who has decided to travel with the herd to the next waterhole.

After walking for several days, Zonda stops to rest late on a very hot afternoon. Tumeleng stays underneath Ayanna and takes a nap. When she wakes up, she looks for Rafiki. He is sitting under the shade of a tree all by himself. As Tumeleng walks over to join him, she sees he is looking at something he is holding with the finger-like tip of his trunk. There are big tears sliding down his face and he is trembling. Alarmed, Tumeleng speaks softly, "Rafiki, what's wrong? Don't you feel well?"

"I'm not sick. It's not that," he sniffles. "I just feel soooo sad."

"I think everyone feels sad lately, Tumeleng said. Those elephants were our friends."

"I know, b-b-but, you don't understand," he sobbed. "That was my family."

Rafiki lifts his trunk to show Tumeleng what he is holding. It is a small bone. "This is all I have left of my m-m-m-m-mother," he cries. "Now I really am an orphan!" Tumeleng gently rubs Rafiki's head with her trunk.

Just then, Zonda signals she wants to travel a few more miles before it gets dark. "There is water up ahead," she announces. When everyone gets in line, Tumeleng and Rafiki walk behind Ayanna and Jabari. While they are walking, Rafiki asks shyly "Will you always be my friend Tumeleng?"

"Of course I will, and what's more, you are not an orphan. You are part of our family now. My Mother told me that she will care for you and teach you until you are big enough to travel with Jabari and his band. That will be a long time from now, so we can always be best friends."

So Rafiki and Tumeleng walk from waterhole to waterhole on their long journey into the future together.

## The End

CPSIA information can be obtained
at www.ICGtesting.com
Printed in the USA
LVHW072322111220
673921LV00003B/76